Fairy magic

Fairy Magic

Cerrie Burnell ✳ Laura Ellen Anderson

SCHOLASTIC

For Amelie, my Autumn Rose.
And for those who believe in fairies.

C.B.

For Rosie. A very special friend
and queen of the bluebells!
'Bug hugs' always xxx

L.E.A.

With special thanks to Vicki Kirwin,
Audiology Specialist for the National Deaf Children's Society

www.ndcs.org.uk

Once there was a girl called *Isabelle*
who lived in a house of a thousand **happy** sounds.

Her big sister *Isla* loved
banging the drums.

BANG
CLASH!

ROCK
AND
DRUMROLL

Her big brother *Ivan*
loved playing football.

GOAALLL!

Her twin brother *Idris* loved pretending to be a purple dragon.

ROOOAAARRR!

Isabelle didn't hear many of these sounds, for her world was filled with echoes and quiet.
So sometimes she wore a listening headband, which brought each sound dancing to her ears.

Or sometimes she pointed out her thoughts with her hands.

When she was with her twin brother Idris, Isabelle needed
no words at all, as he understood her jokes perfectly.

One **very noisy** morning, Isabelle's listening headband
made the world sound sharp, so she took it off and
skipped into the wood of wild flowers.

The calm surrounded her
like a deep soft dream.

Then beneath the sunlit silence came the tiniest tinkling bell – a movement so soft that not even a mouse would have noticed it.

But Isabelle who was used to stillness felt it like a flutter in her heart.

There was a flicker of light,

then a fairy hovered in front of Isabelle on wings of sunshine and grace. "My name is Summer-Blue," the fairy told her.

Isabelle gasped. She could understand
the fairy perfectly. Not hear her, but
feel her words, like a gentle breeze.

"We must awaken the woods for summer," smiled Summer-Blue and together they touched each bluebell, until Isabelle's heart seemed to sing.

Softly the woods began to stir. Baby birds unfurled their wings,
butterflies took flight, and a flock of fairies filled the air
in a whirl of wings and wildflowers.

Isabelle found herself dancing
to the secret song of the woods.

"Look what the fairies gave me,"
Isabelle smiled at supper,
tucking the flowers into
her listening headband.

"There's no such thing as *fairies*," chuckled Ivan.
"They don't exist," cried Isla, and everyone started to laugh.

Isabelle ran upstairs.

Idris followed her and held out his hand.

"Do *you* believe me?" Isabelle asked.

Idris gently shook his head.

The next day Summer-Blue was helping a butterfly dry its wings.

"*None* of my family believe you're real," Isabelle sighed.

"Not everyone can feel our magic the way you can," smiled the fairy.

And she showed Isabelle
something truly wonderful.

"Butterflies sense sound through their **wings**.

Dragonflies can't hear at all – they use their incredible **eyes**.

And **snails** find their way with their sense of **smell**."

"They're just like *me*," Isabelle breathed, her heart **fluttering** with wonder.

"Did you know that butterflies don't hear sound?"
Isabelle beamed at suppertime.
"Who told you that?" asked Ivan.
"Summer-Blue the fairy," Isabelle said.

"*Fairies* don't exist," sighed Isla.

"They do. It's just that *you* can't feel their thoughts,"
Isabelle explained, "because you're not used to silence."

This time nobody laughed.

Every bright day, Summer-Blue taught Isabelle
the secrets of the flowers and bugs.

Idris began to wonder
if Summer-Blue was
real after all.

Then **one morning**, the air was cooler, leaves were falling and the woods were empty and still.

Isabelle ran back to the house. "What's wrong?" her family cried.
"Summer-Blue is *gone*," Isabelle gasped.
Ivan wrapped her in a huge hug.

Isla stroked her hair. "Perhaps she'll be back
next summer?" she mouthed.

Idris knew what to do.
He set off into the woods.

Autumn sunshine surrounded him
like a soft warm cloak and Idris
stood still in the silence.

There was the tiniest flutter of air and Idris held his breath.
Then a fairy appeared on wings of morning mist.

Idris needed to tell his twin. He climbed the nearest tree and **shook** its branches.

Isabelle followed the trail of tumbling leaves...

...and gave her brother a look that needed
no words at all: Thank you.

"I'm Autumn-Rose,"
the fairy told her,
"friend of Summer-Blue.
It's time for summer to sleep
and autumn to awaken."

Isabelle took her brother's hand.
"Let's do it *together*," she smiled, and they
set off happily through the silent trees.

First published in 2017 by Scholastic Children's Books
Euston House, 24 Eversholt Street
London NW1 1DB
a division of Scholastic Ltd
www.scholastic.co.uk
London ~ New York ~ Toronto ~ Sydney ~ Auckland
Mexico City ~ New Delhi ~ Hong Kong

Text copyright © 2017 Cerrie Burnell
Illustrations copyright © 2017 Laura Ellen Anderson

HB ISBN 978 1407 16487 8
PB ISBN 978 1407 16488 5